For Andrew
E.L.

For my friend, Saffron
A.B.

Scholastic Children's Books,
Commonwealth House, 1-19 New Oxford Street, London WC1A 1NU, UK
a division of Scholastic Ltd

London • New York • Toronto • Sydney • Auckland
Mexico City • New Delhi • Hong Kong

First published by Little Hippo, an imprint of Scholastic Ltd, 1999

Text copyright © Elizabeth Laird, 1999
Illustrations copyright © Ailie Busby, 1999

ISBN 0 590 19989 7

Typeset in Goudy Oldstyle

Printed in Italy by Amadeus S.p.A. - Rome

This Little Hippo
book belongs to

_____

_____

King of the Supermarket

by Elizabeth Laird

illustrated by Ailie Busby

It's a fine, bright, beautiful morning and Daniel's going shopping. Saffron's in her buggy, all ready to go, and Grandma's put on her coat and scarf and found her bag and her key. Daniel's got some money left over from his birthday and today he's going to spend it.

"I'm going to buy all the toys in the shop," he says. "Toys! Shop!" says Saffron.

"Mm-mmm," says Grandma, fixing
the bobbles on Saffron's hair.
Grandad looks out of the kitchen.
"Look after your Grandma, Daniel,
in case she gets lost," he says. "All right?"
"All right," says Daniel.
He opens the front door. They're off.

Everybody's out in the street this morning.
What a rumbling of buses and roaring of drills and blaring
of music from the shops!
"I'm going to buy a dumper truck with great big wheels,"
says Daniel.

"Dumper wheels," says Saffron.

"Uh-huh," says Grandma, steering Saffron round
the machine full of bubblegum balls outside the newsagent.
"Oh my, what a crowd! Take hold of the buggy, Daniel.
All right?"

There's a man on the street corner selling radio
cassette players.
"Come on!" he yells. "They're big! They're beautiful!
They're cheap, cheap, cheap!"
"Cheap, cheap, cheap!" says Saffron.

"I'm going to buy one of those," says Daniel.
"I want the biggest one with the round red speakers."
"Oh-oh," Grandma says. "The lights are changing. Now you hold my hand tight, Daniel. We're going to cross the road. All right?"

Here's the supermarket and the doors are wide open.
Grandma and Saffron and Daniel go inside.
It's so big in here!
Everything's bright and gleaming
and busy and clean.
Saffron sees a pile of plums
on the fruit stall near the door.
She grabs one.
"Nice," says Saffron.
"Put that back quick," says Grandma,
"before the lady sees you. Now where do
they keep the biscuits in this place?
And the eggs? And the cakes?"

There are so many people by the
food shelves that there's hardly
any room to breathe.

Arms and legs push and shove
and Saffron starts to grizzle.
Grandma fills her basket.

"It's terrible here, really," says Grandma. "Keep close to me, Daniel. We'll go to the toys in a minute. Saffron! Stop kicking! Your shoes are coming off!"

She bends down to pick up Saffron's shoes
and behind her Daniel sees a row of teddies.
"The toys are just behind you, over there, Grandma!"
he says, tugging at her arm.

"Go and look at them then," says Grandma. "Wait for me right there by the toy shelf while I see to Saffron's shoes. All right?"

Daniel darts across to the shelf of teddies.
But they're not real teddies at all! They're china mugs!
Daniel looks round. He can't see the toy shelf anywhere.
He can't see Grandma and Saffron either.

Daniel's all on his own and he's very, very scared.
He starts to cry and people crowd round and look at him.
"Your mum gone and lost you, has she?" says a man.
"Poor little boy," says a lady. "I'll find her.
Come with me," and she tries
to catch hold of Daniel's arm.
But Daniel knows he mustn't go with
strangers and he pulls his arm away.
"No!" he shouts. "I don't want you!
I only want my Grandma!"

There's a shop man nearby filling shelves from a trolley.
He comes up to see what the problem is.
"Tell you what," he says to Daniel. "If I lift you up
on my trolley, you might be able to see your Grandma.
How about it?"
Daniel stops crying and he nods, and the man
lifts him up and stands him on the trolley.
Now Daniel can see the whole enormous store.
He feels like a king, the
king of the supermarket!
Best of all, he can see
one bright orange scarf
he'd know anywhere.
"Grandma!" yells Daniel.

Grandma turns round at once and rushes up to Daniel,
Saffron's buggy flying through the crowds.

"You naughty child! Where have you been? I've been
waiting and waiting beside the toys!" she says.

"I'm not naughty," cries Daniel. "I thought those teddies
were toys! I thought the toys were here!"

"Oh Daniel," says Grandma. "I'm sorry. You gave me such
a fright, I thought I'd lost you. Now you just get down
from there and we'll get on with our shopping. All right?"

But Daniel's jumping with excitement. Over the heads of all the people he can see the toys, and there, right in the middle of them, is something green and spiky with red googly eyes. It's just what he wanted, all the time.

He lets the man lift him down and then he drags Grandma and Saffron along to the toy shelves.

"Look, Grandma," he says. "That's what I want! A monster!"

Grandma checks the price.

"Looks about right," she says. "You got your money, safe and sound? Let's get along to the check-out."

Daniel picks up the monster and takes out his money and they go along to the check-out and pay the lady.

"Wah!" says Daniel, holding up his monster to frighten the check-out lady.

"Oo!" she says. "You scared me silly."

"Woo-oo!" says Daniel, waggling his monster in front of Saffron, but she just laughs and tries to grab hold of it.

"Let's get along home," says Grandma, "and see how much that monster scares your Grandad. All right?"

"All right," says Daniel.